FIVE LITTLE PUMPKINS

A traditional rhyme illustrated by

Ben Mantle

HarperCollins *Children's Books*

Five little pumpkins
sitting on a gate.

Pumpkin
Patch

This book
belongs to

. . . .

First published in paperback in Great Britain by HarperCollins Children's Books in 2009
This edition published in 2017

3 5 7 9 10 8 6 4

ISBN: 978-0-00-825311-0

HarperCollins Children's Books is a division of HarperCollins Publishers Ltd.

Illustrations copyright © HarperCollins Publishers Ltd 2009, 2017

Visit our website at: www.harpercollins.co.uk

Printed and bound by Bell and Bain Ltd, Glasgow

The first one said,
"My, it's getting late!"

The second one said,
"There are witches in the air!"

The third one said,

"Good folk, beware!"

The fourth one said, "We'll run...

The fifth one
said, "Let's have
some fun!"

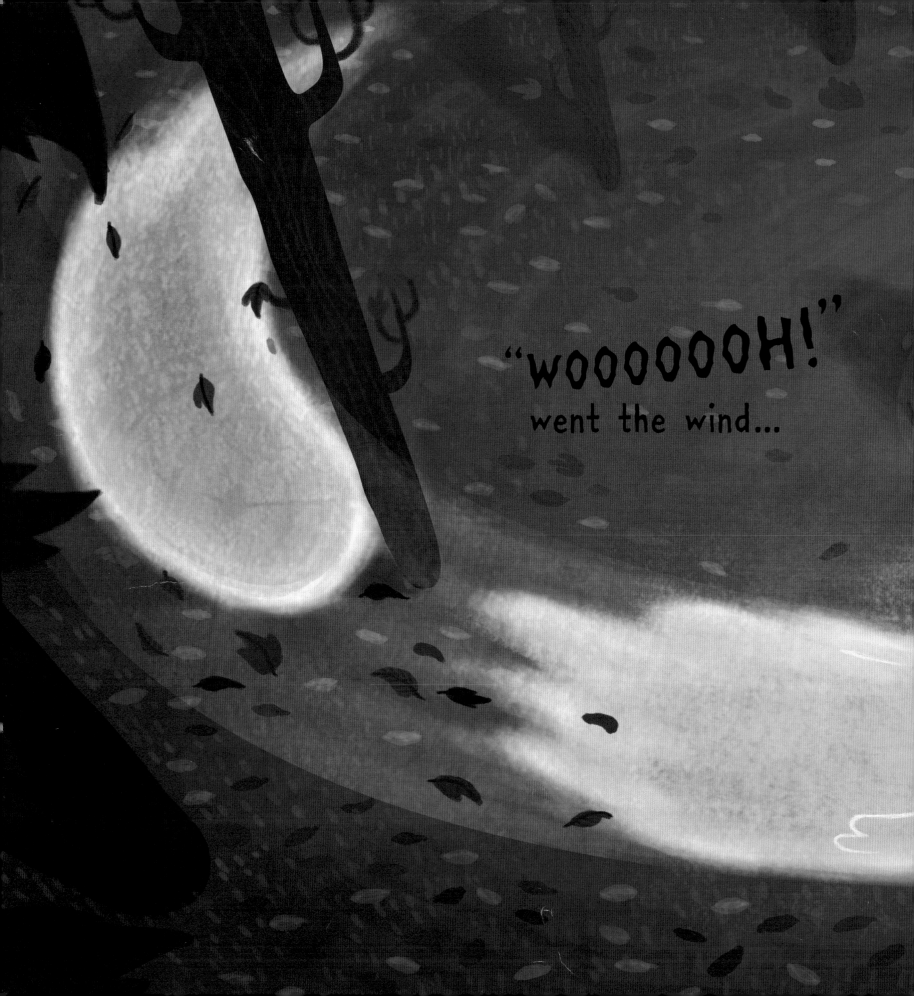

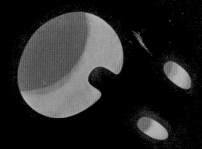

...and OUT

went the light...

...and the
five little pumpkins...

...rolled out of sight!